Dig the Dog

Written by
Alison Maloney

Illustrated by
Maddy McClellan

little bee

Dig the Dog dug and dug,
deep down in the dirt.

By the back door,
Dig the Dog buried
a beautiful,
beefy bone.

Doug the Dog dug and dug,
down in the dusty dirt.

Deeper and deeper Doug dug,
under the garden gate.

Doug the Dog
wriggled and wiggled
into the garden
of Dig the Dog.

Dig the Dog was munching and crunching his best bacon biscuits.

Doug the Dog

Sniffed and Snuffled
and stuck his snout
in the dirt.

Then he dug and **dug**,
until he found
the beautiful **beefy** bone.

Then **Doug the Dog** disappeared under the garden gate.

Dig the Dog finished his food and dug in the dirt for dessert.

He snuffled and **Sniffled** and dug and **dug.**

but the beautiful, bone had gone.

Dig the Dog
squeezed and wheezed
under the garden gate.

Doug the Dog was munching and crunching the beautiful **beefy** bone.

Dig the Dog
growled and
howled
and...

...Doug the Dog
arced and barked.

Doug the Dog sat and spat and...

...**Dig the Dog** scratched and snatched.

Kit the Cat appeared
and sneered at Dig
and Doug the Dogs.

Doug grinned at Dig.
Dig grinned at Doug.

They raced and chased the Cat.

Kit the Cat
span and ran
as Dig and Doug
barked and larked.

They turned and faced the **beefy** bone.

Dig the Dog
licked and picked.

Doug the Dog
chomped and champed.

Until the beautiful **beefy** bone...